WESLEY LEARNS ABOUT INSURANCE

Featuring NFL Hall of Famer Terrell Davis

Prince Dykes, MBA, AFC
and Wesley Dykes

Edited by Andy Multer, MBA
Illustrated by Brandon Avant

ISBN: 978-0-9983-8605-8 (sc)
ISBN: 978-0-9983-8604-1 (hc)
ISBN: 978-0-9983-8603-4 (e)

Library of Congress Control Number: 2019903070

Because of the dynamic nature of the Internet, any web addresses or links contained in this book may have changed since publication and may no longer be valid. The views expressed in this work are solely those of the author and do not necessarily reflect the views of the publisher, and the publisher hereby disclaims any responsibility for them.

Lulu Publishing Services rev. date: 07/02/2019

G.C.F.L.F

Global Children Financial Literacy Foundation

Dedication

To my three older brothers (left to right): Duante Dykes, John Dykes III, Prince Dykes, and LeGregory Dykes Sr.

It was another nice and sunny autumn day as the sun shone through the clouds.

Uncle Rob picked up Wesley from school to take him to soccer practice.

"Wesley, how was school today, and are you ready for practice?" Uncle Rob asked.

"School was great, Uncle Rob, and I was good today. I can't wait for practice!" Wesley replied.

"Awesome!" Uncle Rob exclaimed. "I can't thank you enough for the information that helped me with my credit. I paid off my debt, got a new car, and even started investing. I love this car!"

"Wow! This car is awesome, Uncle Rob. And you're investing now too?" Wesley replied.

"Yes, I've been investing by purchasing S&P 500 index funds and reinvesting the dividends. My investing has done pretty well for me so far," Uncle Rob said.

Out of nowhere, there was a loud noise–bang!–that scared Wesley and Uncle Rob.

"What was that?" Wesley yelled.

"Oh, my goodness! I hit something!" Uncle Rob said.

"Wesley, are you okay?" Uncle Rob asked.

"Yes, Uncle Rob. I'm okay," Wesley said.

"I didn't see that tree behind me!" Uncle Rob exclaimed.

"Can you get your car fixed?" Wesley asked.

"No, and it will cost too much money right now to buy a new one. Call your dad so he can give us a ride to practice," Uncle Rob said sadly.

Wesley was confused about the whole situation but said, "Okay, I will."

"I wish I had insurance," Uncle Rob said.

"What's insurance?" Wesley asked.

"Wesley! Now is not a good time to ask about insurance! Just call your dad now!" Uncle Rob said in frustration.

Wesley then used Uncle Rob's phone to call his dad. "Okay! Dad said he's on his way," Wesley said.

Wesley's dad picked up Wesley and Uncle Rob, and they headed for the children's club for Wesley's soccer practice.

"I'm glad you both are safe! It could have been worse," Wesley's dad said.

"My car ... I just bought it, and now it's wrecked," Uncle Rob said.

"Calm down," Wesley's dad said. "That's what insurance is for. It will give you money to buy a new one."

"I know. I know. But I don't have insurance," Uncle Rob admitted.

"Why don't you have car insurance?" Wesley's father asked.

"I just never got it. I didn't think I would need it, and I didn't want to pay extra for it. Besides, I have never been involved in an accident," Uncle Rob replied.

Wesley was confused and scratched his head, trying to understand what was going on. "Dad, what's insurance?" he asked.

"Insurance?" Wesley's dad repeated. "You really want to learn about insurance? Ha-ha! Maybe another time. We're running late for your practice."

"Oh, my goodness! Is that Terrell Davis?" Wesley's dad asked.

"Where? Are you talking about NFL Hall of Famer and Denver Broncos legend Terrell Davis?" Uncle Rob asked.

"Wow! It is him!" Wesley's dad said.

"Let's go say hi," Uncle Rob suggested.

Wesley's dad and Uncle Rob were shocked to see Terrell Davis. Wesley was with his uncle and dad but looked confused because he didn't know who Terrell Davis was.

"Are you Terrell Davis, the two-time Super Bowl champ and now NFL Hall of Famer?" Uncle Rob asked Terrell Davis.

Terrell Davis laughed and shook Uncle Rob's hand. "Yes, I am. And nice to meet you."

"Wow! Nice to meet you, Mr. Davis. What brings you here today?" Wesley asked.

"Just talking to kids about finance. Since retiring from football, I joined a new team," he said.

"New team?" Uncle Rob asked.

"Yeah, my new team is called Alpha1 Tax and Wealth," Terrell said.

"Alpha1 ... Tax ... what is that?" Wesley's dad asked.

Terrell laughed again. "I'm glad you asked. At Alpha1 Tax and Wealth, we take an educational team approach to retirement planning."

"Oh, I see. What is retirement planning?" Wesley asked.

"We make sure people don't run out of money once they stop working," Terrell said. "We also make sure they have proper insurance in case something happens before or after retirement."

When Wesley heard Terrell Davis mention insurance, a bell went off in his head.

"Insurance ... insurance! Mr. Davis, please tell me—what is insurance?" Wesley asked.

"Wesley! Don't bother Mr. Davis, I will explain later?" Wesley's dad said sternly.

"Ha-ha! It's okay. How about you guys take my card and stop by my office sometime?" Terrell suggested.

Wesley's dad said, "Rob, I can't believe you didn't have insurance on your car. Are you serious?"

"I told you, I didn't think I needed it. Plus, it cost extra money. I've never had a car accident, so I thought I never would," Uncle Rob said.

"Dad, what does it mean that Uncle Rob doesn't have insurance? Does that mean he will get a new car?" Wesley asked.

Wesley's dad took a deep breath. "Well, since we taught you about investing and credit, we might as well teach you about insurance," he said, turning to Wesley's mom.

Uncle Rob said to Wesley's mother in a low voice, "Don't freak out when I tell you this, but Wesley and I were in an accident."

"Accident? Wesley! Are you okay?" she asked.

"I'm okay, Mom, but Uncle Rob lost his new car," Wesley said.

"And he didn't have insurance," Wesley's dad added.

"He didn't have insurance?" Wesley's mom repeated.

"Mom, what is insurance? Why won't anyone tell me Wesley asked.

"Well, it's something you buy, and then, if you ever have an accident, the insurance pays you," Wesley's mom explained.

"What kind of accident?" Wesley asked.

"Any type of accident, Wesley. Remember when Grandma passed away a few years ago? She had life insurance, so Grandpa received some money to pay for her funeral, house, car, and such," Wesley's mom replied.

"Oh, I see. If you have insurance, it pays for things if you die. But Uncle Rob didn't die," Wesley said.

"Wesley, that's true," his dad said, "but that's a different type of insurance. If Uncle Rob had insurance on his car, he could receive money from the insurance company to fix his car or even receive enough money to replace the car if it was too damaged to repair."

"So you can have insurance on a car too?" Wesley said.

"Yes, you can insure almost everything. You know what? Let me call Terrell Davis to set up an appointment," Wesley's dad said.

"Nice to see you guys again. How may I help you?" Terrell Davis asked.

"Can you tell me about insurance?" Wesley asked.

"Ha-ha! I've never seen a kid so interested in insurance. Well, insurance is very important when making a financial or retirement plan. It's something I like to call a game plan. You never know when an accident might happen, and it will wreck your entire plan," Terrell said.

Uncle Rob sat up. "Tell me about it. I had everything going in the right direction. Thanks to my brother and nephew. I finally had fixed my credit and even started investing. Then out of the blue—boom!—I hit a tree. I didn't have insurance on my car, and now I have to use all the money in my savings to get a new car."

"Oh, wow! A simple monthly payment of around fifty dollars could have covered you for a new car, and you would still have enough to save and invest," Terrell said.

"You're right. All the money I saved and invested has to go into buying another car now. If I'd had insurance, I could have received a payout for a new car," Uncle Rob lamented.

"It's a lesson learned. For example, I have insurance on my life, car, business, and house in case something happens. I pay for it every month, but it's worth it if something tragic happens," Terrell said.

"My grandma had life insurance before she passed away," Wesley said.

"Great! It's one of the easiest ways to pass money down to the next generation to create generational wealth," Terrell said.

"This is great information! All right, Wesley, it's getting late, and you have a soccer game tonight," his dad said.

"Oh yeah! Mr. Davis, you want to come and watch my soccer game tonight?" Wesley asked excitedly.

"Sure!" Terrell exclaimed.

Awesome game, Wesley," his dad said.

"Thanks, Dad, but I hurt my ankle," Wesley said.

"Yeah, but it seems you just twisted it a bit. We'll take you to the doctor," Wesley's dad said.

"See, Wesley, that's a form of insurance as well," Terrell Davis said.

"Insurance? How?" Wesley asked.

"Health insurance! See, today you had an accident and hurt your ankle. If your dad didn't have health insurance, it could cost a lot of money to see a doctor," Terrell explained.

"There's insurance for everything," Wesley replied.

"Pretty much! Accidents can happen at any time for any reason," Terrell said.

Wesley scratched his head and thought of his lawn mower. "I wonder if I could get insurance on my lawn mower. I mow lawns to make money, and I couldn't afford to buy a new one if an accident happened," Wesley said.

"You know what, Wesley? You can get personal property insurance," Terrell said.

"Wesley, that might not be a bad idea, especially because you always leave the lawn mower around. Mr. Davis, how can we make this happen?" Wesley's dad said.

"No problem! My team and I will get you a quote tomorrow," Terrell said.

"Thanks, Mr. Davis," Wesley said.

"Wesley, are you ready? Let's go," said Wesley's dad.

"Wesley! Get over here now!" Wesley's dad yelled.

"Yes, Dad?" Wesley said.

"Look outside! I tried to start your lawn mower, and it wouldn't start. Did you hit something with it?" his dad asked.

"Oh no, Dad! I did run over a big stick. How am I going to make money cutting grass if my lawn mower is broken?" Wesley asked.

"Wesley, I told you to take care of your things!" his dad scolded.

"It was an accident, Dad. Wait ... Dad, didn't we get insurance on the lawn mower?" Wesley asked.

"You're right! We did get personal property insurance on your lawn mower," Wesley's dad exclaimed.

"Does that mean I can get a new lawn mower?" Wesley asked.

"Let's go see Mr. Terrell Davis and ask if this is covered," his dad said.

"Wesley, it's nice to see you again. You are in luck because your insurance covers the cost of your lawn mower," Terrell Davis said.

"Oh, wow! I can get a new lawn mower!" Wesley exclaimed.

"If you didn't have insurance, you would have to purchase a new lawn mower with your own money. It was only a premium of five dollars per month for the policy," Terrell said.

"Premium? What is a premium? What is a policy?" Wesley asked.

"Well, Wesley, insurance isn't free. You have to pay for it monthly, semi-annually, or annually. The money you pay for the insurance is called a premium. The policy is pretty much a contract between you, as the policyholder, and the insurance company, saying how much you will pay and what the insurance company will cover, as well as the deductibles," Terrell explained.

"Okay, got it. But what is a deductible?" Wesley asked.

"A deductible is the money a person has to pay toward a claim before an insurance company will pay for the amount covered. Deductibles are in place to stop people from making risky decisions just because they have insurance," Terrell said.

"Oh, okay. So it's like an investment?" Wesley asked.

"Very much so because it helps protect assets, and it can even be used as an investment," Terrell said.

"Insurance as an investment?" Wesley asked.

"Yes, some policies have an investment side attached to them. This is called cash value. Some of the premium will pay for thc policy, and some will go to the cash value. This cash value can be invested into stock indices or loans or pay for the policies. You also have things like annuities that pay money annually," Terrell explained.

"Wow, this is a lot. I thought insurance was just in case I have an accident," Wesley said.

"It is, but insurance is also a very big part of financial planning. At any time, anything can happen to hurt your financial plan. A good example is Uncle Rob's case. He was on the right track, but then—boom—everything changed," Terrell said.

"Thank you, Mr. Davis. Once we receive the money, we will get a new lawn mower," Wesley said.

"Wow! Just like that, I have a new lawn mower. Insurance really saved me a lot of money because I didn't have to use my savings to buy a new one," Wesley said.

"Wesley, I learned a lot too. You can bet I'll get Insurance on my house, car, and life," Uncle Rob said.

"Congratulations, Uncle Rob! You never know when an accident might happen," Terrell said.

"Mr. Davis, do you wear your Hall of Fame jacket everywhere?" Wesley asked.

Everyone laughed.

THANK YOU FOR YOUR SUPPORT!

Special Thanks
Terrell Davis
Theresa Villano
Alpha1 Tax & Wealth
Chadrick Davis
J'mese White

Glossary

Accident Insurance - Insurance for unforeseen accidents causing bodily harm.

Annuity - A fixed sum of money paid to someone each year, in most cases for the rest of the person's life.

Beneficiary - In individual who may benefit from an insurance policy and receive payments.

Cash Value - A form of permanent life insurance that has a cash-value savings account.

Deductible - Portion of the insured loss paid by the policyholder.

Insurance - A contract that transfers risk from a person to a company.

Health Insurance - Insurance the covers bodily damage or sickness, including related medical bills.

Index Annuity - An interest earning fixed annuity tied a major index, for example S&P 500.

Insured - A person or thing covered by an insurance policy.

Life Insurance - A insurance that pays out a sum of money either on the death of the insured person or after a set period.

Personal Property Insurance - Insures the items inside your home, for example as toys, refrigerator, stove and other things that can be damaged or lose.

Policy - A written contract of an insurance agreement.

Premium - Money that is paid for insurance coverage.

Retirement Planning - The process of determining how much income is needed during retirement and the actions need to reach those goal.

About the Author

Prince Dykes was introduced to finance while serving as a logistics specialist on submarines in the US Navy. He earned an associate's degree, bachelor's degree, master of business administration degree, and Series 65 and Series 63 insurance licenses. He became a certified financial educator instructor, as well as an accredited financial counselor while serving in the navy.

In 2013, Prince founded Royal Financial Investment Group and the highly successful YouTube channel podcast, "The Investor Show." In 2015, Prince Dykes published the groundbreaking children's book, *Wesley Learns to Invest*. Prince titled the book after his then-three-year-old son, Wesley Dykes. In 2016, Prince created the cartoon series *Wesley Learns*, adding to the worldwide appeal for financial literacy. He was also a finalist for the ABC hit show *Shark Tank* in season seven but was not selected for the taped showing.

In 2017, Prince Dykes founded the Global Children Financial Literacy Foundation. He also hosted the Hawaii local financial literacy TV show, *The Prince of Investing*. Prince then published his second children's book to teach kids about credit, *Wesley Learns about Credit*. He now has over 150,000 social media followers. His books have been added to over seven public libraries globally and twenty-three public schools.

Prince Dykes's cartoon series, books, and show continue to set the standard for children and parents everywhere who want to learn more about finance.

Prince currently serves in the US Navy. He is also a student at the College for Financial Planning, working toward becoming a certified financial planner. Prince resides in Denver, Colorado, with his wife and their seven-year-old son, Wesley.

About Terrell Davis

Denver Broncos legend, NFL Hall of Famer and entrepreneur, Terrell Davis was born October 28, 1972 and had a historic career from 1995 to 2001. Davis was drafted by the Broncos in the sixth round (196th pick overall) of the 1995 NFL Draft. Davis is the Denver Broncos all-time leading rusher, with 7,607 rushing yards. As a player, he was given the nickname "T. D." by players, fans and the media; this denoted both the initials of his first and last name as well as being an abbreviation for touchdown.

Davis was sent to the Pro Bowl in the 1996, '97, and '98 seasons. Nicknamed "TD," Davis popularized the "Mile High Salute," a military-style salute given to fans and teammates in celebration of a touchdown.

On July 27, 2007, it was announced that Davis would be inducted into the Denver Broncos Ring of Fame. His induction ceremony took place at Invesco Field at Mile High on September 23, 2007, in a Broncos home game against the Jacksonville Jaguars. In 2006, Davis was inducted into the Breitbard Hall of Fame and into the NFL Hall of Fame in 2017. In 2018 he partnered with Alpha 1 Tax & Wealth.